How Many Times Do I Have to Tell You?

Ray Speakman

AuthorHouse™ UK Ltd.
1663 Liberty Drive
Bloomington, IN 47403 USA
www.authorhouse.co.uk
Phone: 0800.197.4150

© *2014 Ray Speakman. All rights reserved.*

No part of this book may be reproduced, stored in a retrieval system, or transmitted by any means without the written permission of the author.

Published by AuthorHouse 07/16/2014

ISBN: 978-1-4969-8677-1 (sc)
ISBN: 978-1-4969-8664-1 (hc)
ISBN: 978-1-4969-8678-8 (e)

Any people depicted in stock imagery provided by Thinkstock are models, and such images are being used for illustrative purposes only. Certain stock imagery © *Thinkstock.*

This book is printed on acid-free paper.

Because of the dynamic nature of the Internet, any web addresses or links contained in this book may have changed since publication and may no longer be valid. The views expressed in this work are solely those of the author and do not necessarily reflect the views of the publisher, and the publisher hereby disclaims any responsibility for them.

Contents

Dedication vii
1 The Bad Word 1
2 The beginnings of a plan 7
3 The Lost Names 11
4 Blame 19
5 Prisoners of War 27
6 An arrow from the shadows. 31
7 Aftermath 35
8 Consequences. 39
9 In hiding 47
10 Endurance 53
11 The Race 59
12 How Many More Times Do I Have to Tell You? 67
13 Multiplex Showdown 77
14 Hard Times 85
15 Victor 91
16 Mission disaster 95
17 What did I tell you? 101
18 It was the computer games. 103
19 A letter from Henley 107

Dedication

For Matilda, Violet, William, Oliver, and their wonderful mum, Hannah, for passing on her love of books.

1

The Bad Word

Now. I know it's a really bad word to use, ever, and my mother would interrupt me with, "How many times do I have to tell you not to use that word?" - but …

I hated this kid. That's the word, hated. "You're using that word again," she would say, but she didn't understand about this kid and how I hated him so much, I used to lie in bed at night hating him. Thinking of ways to hurt him. Mostly with a machine gun. I wanted to mow him down and then stand there nodding – satisfied – savouring the justice of it.

I hated him because he humiliated me in front of my friends – in front of teachers – he humiliated me in the eyes of *myself*. He made me feel useless, powerless, stupid and weak. He seemed to take away my speech so I never knew how to answer him, how to make him stop, how to make him go away.

His favourite sentence was, "Oi – I've been looking for you. I want hold of you."

Then it was – "Come here, come here. What's that in your bag? A book! A booooook! What do you want a book for? Still learning to read? What's this – raw carrots. Look at this, you lot. This kid eats carrots. He's a gerbil."

"Do you mean, rabbit?"

"Don't come funny with me, gerbil, or I'll have to bite you. Got any sweets?"

'No.'

"Liar! What's that in your mouth? Empty your pockets. What's that? Is that off a chocolate bar?

"It's a tissue."

"What, with snot on it? Are you trying to make me touch your snot? Are you trying to make me eat your snot thinking it's a chocolate button?"

"No."

"Right, Chinese burn! Stand still. It won't hurt. It's not hurting is it?"

"No."

"Ha, ha ha... look, you lot, he's going to cry. From a little Chinese burn. A little girl's Chinese burn and he's holding back the little tears. Ahhhhhh!"

And if I did something really stupid like, pushing him away, he'd go – "Oh. Oh. You want to fight me then, do you? You think you can beat me, do you? You think you can triumph over me, do you? What you going to do? Hit me with your book? Stab me with your carrot?"

On and on and on.

"Oi you! What do you think of *Doctor Who?*"

"Brilliant."

"You sad little boy! You actually like *Doctor Who*! Pleeease."

Or

"Oi you! What do you think of *Doctor Who?*"

'Rubbish'

"Rubbish? It's brilliant. I suppose you prefer CBeebies. You tasteless little carrot-eating gerbil."

He was older than me. Next year up in school. His name was Henley Phipps. He lived just near the shops, so I had to pass his house when I went on errands for my mother. Once she sent me for a sliced loaf and he intercepted me, ripped it open and took most of the slices saying he needed the bread for his fishing. Left me with two slices, one was the crust, and an empty wrapper. I pretended to my mum that I had the loaf under my arm and the bread must have fallen out by accident as I walked along. Got sent to bed for that for the rest of the day – 'How many times do I have to tell you to watch what you're doing? You just wait until your Dad gets home, and then you'll know it!'

So lying there in bed, hating, burning with humiliation, seething with indignation – I felt like that bloke in films who gets walked all over again and again by the baddie and then suddenly we all know that the baddie has gone too far and the hero's eyes go steely. He puts a clean shirt on, straps on his gun and walks out into the bright sunlight and the music goes ominous and we all know something terrible is going to happen to somebody, to the baddie obviously, and it does and we feel – yes!!! Retribution! Justice! He deserved it. He *so* deserved it we don't know whether to laugh or cry.

But lying there in bed, sleepless, with the lights of passing cars making patterns on my bedroom ceiling – I knew. No gun. Never mind machine gun, I had no gun of any description. Even if I'd asked for one for my birthday or Christmas, I couldn't see my mum or dad getting me one. "What do want a gun for?" "There's this kid I want to shoot." "You know that killing is wrong, don't you?" "Yeah, but this kid is the exception." "There are no exceptions. Killing is morally wrong." "It's all right for you!!"

Even so. Henley Phipps. Bigger. Louder. Older. Sneerier. How could I make him stop? Go away? Leave me alone? What did I have to do?

****

2

The beginnings of a plan

I had been experimenting with bows and arrows. Straight branch from next door's willow tree sawn off secretly. String from my dad's hardly used shed. Arrows made from garden canes. Feathers from next door but one's pigeon loft – not pulled out, discarded ones and a sharp tip on the cane. I had looked into a poisoned tip but failed to think of anything – so made do with my mother's damson jam. That would kill anybody.

Around my house there were quite high hedges and alongside the house there was an untarmaced road that led to some garages.

A plan was emerging.

Henley Phipps delivered the free paper around about tea-time on a Thursday. When he'd finished he came down our road with a big grey empty bag on his back, usually riding no-handed – showing off – making big 'whey-hey' noises in a 'look at me - coooool' sort of way.

The plan was to wait behind the hedge with my bow and arrow. It would be dusk, twilight and I would be crouched in the shadows, a stealthy thing. He would ride noisily down our road – whey-hey – ooo ooo – no handed me – admire me – and I would take aim a few feet in front of him to allow for the velocity of his hardly in control bike and the arrow would shiver irredeemably towards him – arc Robin Hood-like towards its target. Henley Phipps's heart. If he had one. And he would fall, in slow motion and hit the ground so that windows would shake up and down the street. And as he lay there dying I would walk over to him nodding, satisfied with the justice of it, with a grim but slightly tired look on my face, almost sorry that I had had to do it, and he would say, "You! You!" – and I would reveal no emotion before slipping away silently into the shadows. Incognito. A story forever told in those neat suburban streets.

It was a good plan. I would do it without delay.

****

3

The Lost Names

In my class there were four of us who sat on the same table: Eric, Arthur, Victor and me, Jim. Our theory was that we had been put together because our names were names that time had forgotten: lost names in fact. Names that made people look at us in a slightly puzzled or perhaps pitying sort of way. Eric, Arthur and Victor who was a girl - real name possibly Victoria - but because there are lots of girls called Victoria she had to be Victor so that she could be one of the lost names club. Anyway, she preferred it.

My name, Jim, was probably the most normal of the group, but that was all spoiled by my second name – McConkey. When I had to say my name out loud, which I tried to avoid at all costs, the person receiving this information would struggle not to laugh. Nothing would happen to their face that you could see, but you just knew they were screaming with laughter inside their heads. With Eric, Arthur and Victor, they saw old people disguised as children; with me I think they saw noses. I must have been descended from a long line of large noses – although the one on my face is normal – I think.

Actually I ought to add that with Eric they also saw hair (red, tangled and long) that was too big for his body; with Arthur, a smile (gap-toothed) that was too big for his head and with Victor, with surprised eyes that were too big for her face. For about five minutes we thought of calling Eric, Eric the Red, after the Viking we did a project about once, but we didn't dare call Victor ET – a kid in our class called her this once and then really, really wished he hadn't. Arthur was just Arthur.

Our teacher was called Mr Hetherington. The older kids referred to him as Kenny Hetherington, which we thought qualified him for the lost names club as no one we knew was called Kenny. We didn't invite him to join though, partly because he was a teacher but more than that, he was a very inconsistent shaver. Beard one day, gone the next. Clean face today, dirty face tomorrow.

It was this inconsistent shaving fact that made my Henley Phipps plan become even more urgent.

On this particular day we were just trudging in from playtime, when we noticed that Mr Hetherington was already in the classroom. Normally he arrived after us still drinking his playtime cup of coffee or tea or beard vitamins or whatever it was he drank. On this day he was there with his back to us, looking out of the window. This was ominous and as a result we were subdued.

Unexpectedly, he spun around and looked at us all. With contempt.

"How many times do I have to tell you lot about health and safety?" he said, his look of contempt melting into a look of deep sadness. "This was on my desk this morning!"

He held something up for us all to see. We stood on tiptoes and shifted position to try and see what it was. He walked around the room with his arm stretched high, looking at each person closely as he passed. Once he had moved away from each table we all looked at each other, puzzled.

"Your pretend puzzlement is transparent," he sneered, "You know what I'm talking about. One of you in particular knows what I'm talking about. You know full well that this is a safety razor used for shaving and this morning, it appeared on my desk."

He slapped his hand down on the desk. We jumped.

"Anonymously." Hits the desk again.

"Pointedly." Points a finger at us.

"How many times do I have to tell you about commenting on a person's appearance? Let alone health and safety."

Ray Speakman

There was silence

"I want the person or persons responsible to come out to the front. Now."

We all looked round to see who would come out. Pause. No one.

Mr Hetherington put his hand in his pocket and took out his mobile phone.

"Do I have to?" he said holding out the phone.

We knew what this meant. He was going to phone Mr Nixon, the Deputy Headteacher. His first name *really* had been forgotten, even by his mother. He was old and spiky and seriously scary. Hairless too. Mr Hetherington had too much hair – and today was a particularly bad day – but Mr Nixon had none. Not even up his nose. Or in his ears. We thought he had cobwebs up his nose, but didn't want to look too closely.

"Mr Nixon?" he said into his phone. "Yes – they've had their chance. No. I think you can bring him in now?"

Bring who in? A policeman? A barber? What?

Mr Nixon walked into our classroom leaving the door open behind him. His shoes clicked like tap dancers' shoes and glinted in a beam of dust-laden sunlight. After a brief nod to Mr Hetherington, he turned and looked at us one by one – as though each of us had hugely offended him.

"No answer was the stern reply," he said making a noise that was supposed to sound like a laugh, but didn't. Then he shouted towards the door. "You out there! Step inside if you will."

He always made a point of emphasising the last letters of any word so that 'reply' sounded like 'reply-ya' and 'will' sounded like will-la'.

In through the door, as though he'd been called up onto the stage during assembly to receive a special prize, stepped Henley Phipps. We all froze.

Mr Nixon took the safety razor from Mr Hetherington's hand and held it centimetres from Henley's face.

"Do you recognise thisssss, Henley?"

"Yes, sir."

"Did you see who placed -d it on Mr Hetherington's desk-ka?"

Somehow, the air seemed to have been sucked out of the room.

"Yes, sir."

"And do you see that person or persons in this room- ma, Henley?"

"Yes sir. Definitely, sir. There. Them."

He pointed towards our table.

"Jim, Arthur, Eric and Victor. My office. Now-wa. Thank you, Henley, off you go -wa."

"Do you want me to write a statement, sir?"

"That will not be necessary, Henley. I have them now-wa. Thank you, Mr Hetherington -na."

The class looked on as we left the room thankful that it was us and not them being marched away to our fates.

How Many Times Do I Have to Tell You?

****

4

Blame

Mr Nixon always used the same prelude to a questioning session: waiting. The four of us were left in the corridor outside his office with a two metre gap between each of us - waiting. Eric and Arthur stared straight ahead, clearly scared and Victor kept shooting accusatory glances at me.

"What?"

"Don't 'what' me, Jimmy McConkey," hissed Victor. "It's not me who's antagonised Henley Phipps."

She knew I hated being called Jimmy. Jimmy suggested a little kid. I wanted to be Jim, big Jim, thoughtful Jim, strong Jim. "I didn't set out to antagonise him," I said weakly.

"Shut up, you two. This is serious," said Eric without altering the direction of his stare.

"Someone told me that there are dead kids in Nixon's stockroom," whispered Eric.

Arthur's head swivelled, the colour appearing to drain from his lips. "Is that true?"

Eric shrugged, "It's what I heard."

"Honestly. Say honestly. If it's true, you've got to say, honestly." He was going to cry, I knew he would cry. 'Arthur', I was thinking, 'please do not cry'.

All I could think to say was: "Eric, Arthur, Victor and Jim – based on characters originally created by Alexander Dumas. Remember? One for all and all for one."

Arthur took a breath, Eric nodded and Victor gave me the slightest hint of a smile.

The door at the end of the corridor burst open. A flat-bed trolley appeared, laden with boxes of fruit and pushed by a grinning Henley Phipps.

"Get your healthy playtime snacks. Get yourself a healthy apple or banana, children. It'll put *hairs* on you chin. Watch the trolley! You collide with this trolley and you'll be in serious trouble. *More* serious trouble, I should say. Stand aside. Ooh that was a close *shave*, little Jimmy, missed you by a *whisk*er. Healthy playtime snacks, coming up…"

And he was gone, his laugh echoing down the empty corridor.

"The safety razor on Mr Hethington's desk was definitely him," said Victor. "The question is, why does he want to get us into trouble? Does he hate us or what?"

"He definitely hates me, and I really, really don't know why!" I said.

Mr Nixon's office door opened and a voice bellowed, "Eric. In!"

Eric looked alarmed, turned to us, pointed at his chest and mouthed, "Me?"

"Yes, you," hissed Victor and Eric went in through the door looking very, very small.

For a moment there was silence and then a sharp, loud and very raised voice which sounded more than anything like a bark.

"Has he got a dog in there or is that him barking?" Arthur was not trying to make a joke. He was horrified.

Silence. The door opened. No sign of Eric. "Victor. In!"

Victor put her head down and walked with determination into Mr Nixon's office. Absolute silence. No barks. Not even the sound of a distant teacher's voice not knowing when to stop talking.

"No barks," said Arthur.

"No one barks at Victor. She's bark-proof."

Arthur looked at me. "What's he done with Eric? Do you think… the stockroom…you know?"

"No. He's a bright kid, Eric. This school needs him for the SATs results."

"*I'm* not bright."

"Yes you are, Arthur. You've just got …"

"Undiscovered depths?"

"Exactly! Potential"

"That's a good word. I'll tell my mum."

The door again. No sign of anyone, just that voice again, "Arthur. In!"

And I was alone. Alone, alone, all all alone, alone on a wide, wide sea! Well, a wide, wide corridor anyway. Nothing. No barking. No crying. No gunfire, no swords clashing. No …

"Mr McConkey!" He didn't even open the door, he just bawled through it! I don't think the door actually shook, but it must have nearly been blown off its hinges. "Mr McConkey. I want you in here. Now!"

Mr Nixon sat behind his desk writing. Eric, Victor and Arthur were in a line facing him. I sneaked a sideways look at them as I joined the line. Nothing. Not a flicker. Mr Nixon put down his pen, leaned back in his chair and looked at us.

"I have a complete-ta pictuuuure. I need to ask a – nothing-ga more. I have a witnesssss. I have tesssstimony. I have confessions -sa. I have my own very considerable common sense. And – I have a precise-a and fierce desire to adhere to school rrrules. Beards, stubble, inconsistent shaving, as you will no doubt be able to confirm – are a human right. Safety razors are a weapon and no one, absolutely no one, will be allowed on board this school for its flight into the future with a safety razor in their possession. Mr McConkey, your friends tell me that you are, in effect, the ring leader."

I gasped; looked along the line. Eric and Arthur had their eyes closed. Victor had made her mouth into a tight straight line.

"But it's not true. It wasn't me!" When these sentences came out I was horrified to hear how high my voice was and how I sounded as though I was about to explode into tears. I tried to calm my voice: "It wasn't – it really wasn't. Ask them."

"I *have* asked them. I have questioned them – in detail – and they have revealed all. I have interpreted their combined utterances, and they ADD UP! TO GUILT!" he shouted, roared, exploded – actually – barked, in a way they told you to close your eyes and not even to think of saying another word. "As you know," he was whispering now, "I usually punish-sha wrongdoers with time out to think about what they have done, but in your case – I think a more public punishmentttt."

Eric made a choking noise. Arthur breathed a hardly perceptible whimper. Victor stood up straighter. It was as though they were bracing themselves for a firing squad.

"Eric, Arthur and Victor: three playtimes litter-picking in full overalls, with black bin bag and litter picking sticks. James McConkey, as ringleader, instigator and mastermind – five playtimes – two of them utterly, utterly alone for all to see. Thank you. Mr Hetherington is expecting you back in class. Thank you."

"But I'm innocent!"

Mr Nixon barked out some unintelligible words that sounded like, 'aagghhhh', stood up and banged his hands on his desk. We scuttled out.

How could they? My best friends. What had happened to all for one and one for all? When we had gone through the doors at the end of Mr Nixon's corridor, Victor stopped.

"Hang on."

I made to push past them and head on towards our classroom.

"Jim. Stop. Just listen a minute."

I stopped but didn't say anything. The truth was I couldn't. If I'd tried to say anything, I would have cried. I felt so sorry for myself, so hurt, so misunderstood, so betrayed, so dobbed in! By my best friends!

With one hand on my shoulder so that I could not stride off, Victor slowly explained. "We didn't say it was you, Jim. We said *someone* must have done it to *get* at you. We didn't say who, of course, we're not suicidal, and we just said that we thought it was all caused by someone really hating you!"

"All Nixon heard was us saying it was caused by you. We never said you did it," said Eric.

"Honestly. Look I've said honestly and that means we're telling the truth." Arthur's look said, please believe what I'm saying or I will quite possibly wet myself.

****

5

Prisoners of War

We survived. Despite the sniggers, despite the turning away looks of disgust, despite the huge increase in litter because we were now the servants of the whole school put there to save them the effort of reaching for a bin. It was as though they were saying, "If we put our litter in a bin, Nixon would have us for ruining his carefully planned punishment. Self-protection and anyway we like Mr Hetherington – so – anyway, serves you right!"

Eric spent three playtimes pretending to be a lorry, with a great big steering wheel. He would drive up to the litter, circle it – huffing and puffing in his effort to turn the massive steering wheel - then back up making a beeping sound, put the brake on, pick the litter up with his litter picking stick and then lower the item into his black bin bag. Slinging the bag over his shoulder, he would crash the lorry into gear and roar around the playground looking for more.

Arthur, on the other hand, rode around the playground on an imaginary horse pretending that each piece of litter was a Jabberwocky (a poem he was fixated with). He would wave his litter picking stick at people, particularly if they were little, and shout:

"Beware the Jabberwock, my son,

The jaws that bite, the claws that catch!

Beware the Jubjub bird, and shun,

The frumious Bandersnatch!"

And when the bell went for lessons to start again, he would stand in the middle of the playground turning in circles and shouting: 'O frabjous day! Callooh! Callay!'– and stagger to the big bins with his haul of litter. The little kids laughed and ran away; the bigger kids just thought he was mad but Arthur didn't care.

Meanwhile Victor and I were quite pleased that Eric and Arthur were drawing everyone's attention. We tried to keep our heads down and have a quite conversation as we diligently collected litter.

"Why didn't you dob me in to Nixon, then?"

It was Henley Phipps, suddenly appearing from behind the big bins.

"Cos that's not what you do, is it?" said Victor.

"I'm asking McConkey, not you, little girl. Why didn't you dob me in, McConkey? Is it cos you're scared of me? Is it cos you know if I had a fight with you, you'd get splattered all up the walls?"

I had to say something. "Nobody fights anymore. It's not cool, Henley."

"Who says I'm not cool? Just because I'm not in a gang of kids who've all got weird granddad names, you think I'm not cool? If I wanted to be in a gang like that, I could be. I've got an unusual name. No one in this school or even on this whole estate is called Henley. So I could join a weird names gang if I wanted."

Victor couldn't resist: "Henley is a place name, not a forgotten name. You don't qualify."

I thought Henley was going to start biting her. His teeth came out and he started to dribble and punch the air: "Qualify? Qualify? I'll show you qualify. I don't need to qualify. I don't need no gang. I'm gang all on my own. I'm the biggest most frightening gang this school has ever seen. And violent? You don't know what violent is. Cool or not I can be very violent – and anyway, I've heard there's a kid in Year 1 called Arthur, so all those lost names are on the way back in. Then where will you be, when they're not lost any more?? When all the registers in all the classes are full of granddad names? Beaten up, that's where you'll be. By me! On my own and without any gang of weird-name-losers backing me up!"

"Henley!" It was Mr Nixon. "Lessons, Henley. I think you'll find they are well under way. And you two – move-a."

We moved.

Eric, running to keep up with Victor said, "Victor, did you see Henley's teeth then? Do you think he's turning into a vampire?"

Arthur was appalled: "Honestly? Do you think he is? Say 'honestly'!"

"Never mind turning," I said. "I reckon he's already turned into a vampire. We'll have to watch our necks!"

Just as we were about to go back into class, Victor stopped me and said, "What was that thing you were on about with the bow and arrow?"

"You're right! Something definitely has got to be done."

****

6

An arrow from the shadows.

My dad hadn't come home from work and I told my mum I was going to my bedroom to read.

"If you're going to fall sleep, make sure you switch the light off first. How many times do I have to tell you about the electricity bill?"

"My bulb's got a long life."

"Which is more than you'll have if you don't do as you're told!"

When all was quiet I switched my light out, waited and then slipped, a stealthy shadow, down the stairs, through the kitchen and out into the twilight – and towards my destiny. The light was seeping away like milk into a bowl of cereal. It was getting colder and I knew that I was all but invisible as I glided into position behind the hedge. No sound. No sight. No tell-tale tracks. No mercy. It would be done.

The street was silent: everyone indoors watching the news or eating their teas. Hardly a breeze, temperature sinking and me, rehearsing in my mind the arrow, the death, the tragic look on my face – his realisation of his crimes too late – and my escape back through the shadows to my bedroom.

And then, before I had time to remember which book I was going to read when I got back to my bedroom, he was there, looming out of the twilight.

"Whey – hey – whey heyyyyyyy." Arms spread, no hands, all the time in the world – he thought.

I drew back the string of my bow, I aimed – about two metres ahead of him – so that his heart and the arrow would meet with deadly precision – and – I let go.

It went – like – with more strength than I thought I had, whistling, quivering towards my enemy – arcing – speeding – with me mumbling: "No no no no - I didn't mean it – stop!!" It really was going to kill him! "Mummy, mummy, mummy I didn't mean it."

I couldn't look. I couldn't stop looking. The arrow quivered towards Henley Phipps's heart – and then at the last moment it lost speed and dipped – right through the front wheel of his bike! It was as though he'd hit a brick wall. The arrow stopped his front wheel dead and he, arms wide, mouth open with the "whey-hey" frozen on his lips – headed up into the air.

Before he hit the ground I was gone – down the lane, through the hedge, bow chucked down the garden, through the back door and up to my room – into bed – clothes still on – hiding in the dark under the duvet with a picture in my head of Henley Phipps frozen in the air, arms out, mouth agape and a look on his face that said, "This is going to really hurt".

****

7

Aftermath

I didn't even dare look at the lights making patterns on my bedroom ceiling. The night went on and on. Under the duvet I imagined the voice of the local news reader: '…and the police are appealing for witnesses. His mother, Mrs Phipps was too upset to speak to our reporter but said that the whole family were devastated, just devastated…' Henley's many friends and admirers have been visiting the scene of the accident all day to lay flowers. Police are puzzled by what appears to have been an arrow through the front wheel of the tragic bicycle and are offering a substantial reward for information'.

Although there was no way anyone at all could connect me with the events of the night before, something told me the next morning that I'd better be ill.

"Mum, I think I'm ill."

"What's up with you?"

"I'm seriously ill."

"Where?"

"Everywhere."

"Which part of everywhere?"

"In my body. I think I might be contagious to everybody I meet. I might cause an epidemic."

"Of what?"

"People being ill, of course."

"Get dressed, you're going to school".

"You'll have blood on your hands".

"Yes – yours – if you don't get ready for school," and she stormed out of my bedroom.

"You never believe me," I shouted after her. "You'll be sorry. You know what they'll say. They'll say any normal mother would have put him in quarantine. He should have gone to an isolation hospital, a sanatorium up in the Alps. And now, look what you've done – a whole school will be sent to bed or hospital - suffering. All because of your failure to trust and care for your only son. "

My bedroom door was flung open – hard. "Look! If you're going to pretend to be ill at least get some facts to back up your story. Epidemic? Sanatorium in the Alps? That is just so pathetic, Jimmy! You know how to use a computer, for goodness sake! Look up some proper symptoms next time you want to skive off school. Now get up. Quick - or I'll get a cold flannel!"

How was I to know she could hear me whinging on about her failures as a mother? *And she called me Jimmy!*

8

Consequences.

Downstairs, nothing. Silence. Despite the fact that my nose seemed to be swollen with guilt and my eyes puffy through lack of sleep, my mother said nothing – just slid a bowl of porridge under my nose and got on with her jobs. She was always rushing about in the morning because in the afternoon she worked at the Lime Avenue optician's as a receptionist. I reckon it was there she got fixed up with eyes in the back of her head.

There was definitely something else though. While I was having my breakfast she didn't make eye contact once. All she did was give me my porridge, have a whispered telephone conversation with my dad, who had already left the house, and then rush about getting the house and herself ready for the day. There was something on her mind. I just hoped it had nothing to do with arrows and attempted murder.

When I left for school, the street was empty. No flowers. No wreckage. No flashing blue lights. Nothing.

Well – ha! I'm going to be all right. No horrible consequences. No recriminations – police interviews – on the news with a blanket over my head – no newspaper headlines calling me a monster. Back to normal. I remain – incognito. A shadowy figure, still.

'What did you do?'

It was Jennifer Greenhouse just coming out of her gate.

'I don't know what you mean.'

'What did you do to Henley Phipps?'

'Nothing' – my voice went very high. I had to stop it doing that.

'I saw him this morning when I went to the shops for my mum. He says he wants hold of you. He's telling everybody he wants hold of you. I heard him telling some kids he wants hold of you. You realise he's a vampire, don't you? When he walks past mirrors – nothing – no reflection. You look.'

"Hold of me? Why? That sounds like something no one says any more. Wants hold of me? Me?" almost squeaking and trying to ooze disbelief.

'He didn't say. Just limping in and out of the shops saying he wants hold of you.'

'Limping?'

She shrugged.

By the school gate Eric and Arthur were waiting for me with serious and concerned expressions.

'Eric says you've had it now.'

'I wouldn't like to be you.'

'See – you've *really* had it now.'

'I don't know what you're talking about. I haven't done anything. Any way I was reading all last night. Ask my mum. What's been said?'

They shrugged.

Victor arrived at a run. She pointed at me and said, without even smiling, "Right. We need to talk. Eric and Arthur, come on, we need you for this."

Eric and Arthur looked a bit nervous.

Deep into the school conservation area, which is what they called a weedy part of the school field down in the corner by the main road, we stood in a circle and waited for Victor to speak. There used to be a pond somewhere here once, so people said, but it was lost now – like our names – like us, in fact.

"You did it, didn't you, Jim?"

"Who told you?"

Eric bent forward clasping his head in his hands. "Nooooo! I don't believe it! Tell me it wasn't you, Jimmy."

"I never said I did it. Anyway, my name is Jim," I said sulkily.

Victor took control. "Never mind Jim, Jimmy, any minute now you won't have a name of any sort. And neither will we! We're all dead; you realise that, don't you? Dead. Assassinated. Exterminated. Annihilated."

Arthur, trying to lighten the mood, piped up, "We gave one hundred people sixty seconds to give us a synonym for 'dead'. All you have to do is to find the most obscure answer...."

"For goodness sake, Arthur, this isn't a quiz show. It's not funny!"

"He won't tell Nixon," I said.

"Never mind Nixon, it's Phipps I'm worried about. Nixon wouldn't actually kill you – but Phipps – he's out of control when he's being normal. How could you?"

Arthur's mouth fell open. "How could he what?"

"But how does everyone know it was me? It was dark," I said.

"It was also right outside your house, Jim," Victor said with more than a trace of pity in her voice. "Who else would it be?"

"Oh! Ahhhh! I didn't think of that."

"Did you also not think that what you were doing was just wrong?"

"What was he actually doing?" Arthur again.

"Trying to kill Phipps with a bow and arrow."

"Honestly? Say honestly!"

Eric wrapped his arm around Arthur's neck. "How many times do I have to tell you to listen, Arthur? What do you think everyone's on about? Why do you think every kid we meet is pretending not to see us and scuttling off around the nearest corner?"

Eric looked at me.

"It's me, Arthur, not you. I've caused it."

"After what you said about violence not being cool! How many times have we said that kids who want to fight are just losers? And with a bow and arrow, for goodness sake! We're not Native Americans in the nineteenth century or Robin Hood in the Middle Ages."

"But I said about it before and you said something had to be done."

"No, it was you who said that. And anyway, I thought you were playing, like Arthur and his Jabberwocky 'whiffling through the tulgey wood' with his eyes on fire or us being the musketeers in a story. I thought it was your imagination again! Not real. You can't *really* hurt people, Jim. Not in real life."

"They do on the news."

"We're not on the news. Yet! And have you thought what would have happened if you *had* actually killed him with an arrow? What do you actually think the consequences would have been?"

"I would have got revenge."

"You would have got years and years locked up in a prison because they would have tracked you down – mainly because the arrow was fired from outside your house, for goodness sake, not to mention all the forensic evidence you've probably left all over the place! Flipping heck, Jim, even Henley Phipps seems to have worked it out and that's saying something!"

Eric was becoming more and more alarmed by all this talk of long prison sentences. "But he's not dead is he? Henley Phipps. He's just after Jim, isn't he? And us, probably. He won't report it – he'll just kill us and then *he'll* get sent to prison for years and years."

Victor nodded. "You're right Eric. All we've got to do is lay low for as long as it takes. Then perhaps he'll forget about it. Don't worry, Jim. It'll be all right. In the end."

Wading through the conservation area back into school, none of us was convinced that it would be all right.

Life, as we knew it, was wiffling away from us, as Arthur would say.

****

9

In hiding

It turned out Henley Phipps wasn't at school that day. My mother had bumped into him and his mother waiting at the bus stop. He looked as though he was grinding his teeth, she said, and his face was all bruises. He said he knew who had done it and was going to kill them.

I told my friends. 'I'm not scared,' I kept saying. 'Anyway I haven't done anything to be scared of!'

They all just looked at me. Half fearful. Half pitying.

Mr Hetherington did an assembly about how it was okay to be little, or big, or red- headed, or disabled, or from another country, or old, or poor. He didn't say anything about having a beard or trying to kill someone with a bow and arrow.

With the help of the thoughtful Victor, the poetic Eric and the confused Arthur, we spent playtime in the classroom making a list headed:

Ways to Hide and Keep Positive:

1. Leave home either very early or very late.
2. Me, Victor, Eric and Arthur take it in turns to call for each other before school.
3. All of us travel to school on our scooters. Go as fast as possible and don't look to the left or the right – unless for traffic, of course.
4. Make a list of projects we would like to do as a team. Include:

    - a time plan (years rather than weeks);
    - working spaces (mostly the classroom at every play and lunch time);
    - what the outcome would be (classroom and main hall displays and a whole class presentation at the end);
    - thoughts on how and who would assess the project (including numerous continuous assessment visits by senior members of the teaching staff). We impressed ourselves with this one.
    - A final decision on the exact nature of the area to be investigated and reported on would be left to the teachers: Eric proposed a project on heavy goods vehicles; Arthur thought a giant mobile of a Jabberwocky for the main hall would be quite good, supplemented by lists of made up or composite words, some from Lewis Carroll, some home-made.

Victor and I didn't mind as long as it was about stories. We were willing to take advice from the teachers but reserved the right to make our own final decision – on the grounds that what teachers thought a good read was sometimes a bit suspect – or boring - or a bit too full of SATs[1]-speak. Like 'skim reading'! We didn't want to do skimmed reading, or even semi-skimmed reading. We wanted full fat reading!

5. See Mr Hetherington about the four of us making fulsome recompense for the safety razor incident, and - even though we were innocent and severely wronged by the accusation and punishment - offer to make a wholehearted contribution to the smooth and efficient running of the school community - viz: helping the caretaker by putting out, stacking, repairing and/or removing chewing gum from chairs; setting up an emergency response team to help the little kids with reading, writing, sums and any other mystery of learning, and offering weekend and holiday rest and recuperation facilities to the various stressed school hamsters, guinea pigs and hens.

"I don't know about that last one," said Arthur. "Don't you think we ought to ask our mums and dads first?"

---

[1] Just in case you are reading this lost journal hundreds of years into the future, SATs were Standard Assessment Tests which all kids had to do to find out how much they didn't know.

Victor laughed, "I'd have thought your mum and dad would be quite relieved if you turned up with a real animal instead of going on about Jabberwocks and Jubjub birds."

Mr Hetherington came into the classroom with his usual mug of something in one hand and half eaten piece of something else in the other. "What-ho, lads – and girl. Were you looking for me?"

Victor spoke first: "We wanted to say how fantastic that assembly was this morning, sir."

"Brillig," added Arthur.

"What?"

"And frabjous! Lewis Carroll words, sir – I save them for special occasions."

"Oh – great – really? I'm so pleased you liked it."

"More than liked it. We were inspired by it," continued Victor, "especially Eric with his red hair and everything."

"Yeah, cool," nodded Eric.

"So we wanted to talk to you about some ideas we've had about work and school and things…"

How Many Times Do I Have to Tell You?

"Fantastic. Really? Eric's red hair. I see. Ummm!"

It was like we were building castle walls and a moat all around us made of activities and jobs and model pupil behaviour. As long as we were at school we would be armour-plated. Henley Phipps would not be able to get near us.

****

10

Endurance

By the end of that first day the doughty band of lost names had made surprising progress. The caretaker, Mrs Ditchfield, was quite happy to go along with the various sorts or chair assistance (especially chewing gum removal) and Mr Hetherington mad-keen to come up with an all-consuming topic for us to lose ourselves in. We would have to wait for a staff meeting to discuss the emergency response team to help the little kids, which was okay, we had plenty to get on with. (The offer to take the school pets home, to give them a break from kids staring at them and over-feeding them, was quietly dropped on the grounds that it would take up too many hours of begging and whining to get our families to agree.)

Nevertheless, our defences were almost in place.

At lunchtime Mr Hetherington gave us a copy of a newspaper advertisement from 1914 which read:

MEN WANTED for hazardous journey, small wages, bitter cold, long months of complete darkness, constant danger. Safe return doubtful, honour and recognition in event of success.

Ernest Shackleton 4 Burlington Street

"*Men* wanted?" sneered Victor.

"It *was* 1914. He would have taken girls if it was now," insisted Arthur whose imagination was clearly beginning to abandon Jabberwockys in favour of 'darkness and constant danger'.

"Shackleton's ship was called *Endurance*," enthused Mr Hetherington.

I almost exploded. "Orrr, come on, Vic, this is brilliant! *Endurance*!!! It's perfect"

"Did he take any heavy vehicles with him – for the hazardous journey?" ventured Eric.

Mr Hetherington handed us a book full of pictures. "He had his ship which was fantastic and loads of sledges and dogs."

"Sledges and dogs? No lorries?" A new concept for Eric.

"Not in 1914, no. But -" went on Mr Hetherington as though he was about to reveal an earth-shattering secret, "he had the most amazing photographer with him, called, Frank Hurley. And there are diaries and all sorts…"

Eric put his hand up, "Frank's a good name, sir, isn't it?"

"And can you read the diaries and can you still see all the photos?" said Victor beginning to see possibilities.

"Yes."

Silence. Victor was hooked and the rest of us were lost in thought.

"Tomorrow we could perhaps meet and talk about how we can build in a bit of target-setting aimed at lifting some of your Reading and Writing SATs levels?[2] What do you think?" said Mr Hetherington tentatively.

"O frabjous day! Callooh! Callay! We'll be there, chortling in our joy," whooped Arthur.

"Sorry, sir," said Victor. "Arthur's words again, sir, you know?"

"He wouldn't use those words in a SATs test, would he?"

---

[2] SATs levels: these were the categories children were labelled with after taking the test. Level 6 was the best you could get, which was like the lift taking you up right up to roof level. If the lift was out of order though, everyone ended up in the basement.

"We'll rein him in, sir. Don't worry. Once he's safely on board the *Endurance* he'll start using proper words, no trouble."

At the end of the day, the four of us hung around in the classroom until everyone had gone.

"Fancy doing a bit of marking for me?" laughed Mr Hetherington.

"Yes please!"

"I was joking, Arthur!"

"Oh!"

Henley Phipps had not appeared at all that day and of course we were worried that he would be out there somewhere, in those unsupervised streets, waiting to pounce. Clearly we had school taped. He wouldn't get near us between registration and home time – but – the journey to and from school was another matter. Talk about 'constant danger' and 'safe return doubtful'!

In the end, we had to shuffle out.

"Good night, lads."

"Mmmm!"

The streets were quiet. Too quiet, as they often say in films. Although I didn't actually see anyone, I felt certain that there were kids everywhere watching us. Expectantly. Fearfully. Eyes peering through hedges and from behind curtains; it half-seemed that kids were ducking out of sight behind trees and parked cars. The people in passing cars seemed to be looking at us as though they recognised us, but when we looked back they swiftly turned their heads away. Loads going on just in the corner of your eye but nothing you could actually point at and say, "There!"

I'm sure Eric, Arthur and Victor felt the same, but we said nothing.

And so we made our way home.

****

11

The Race

By the next morning my scooter was ready for the headlong dash from home to school: oiled, greased and polished. Quite a few kids came to school on their scooters – we even had a special scooter rack next to the empty bicycle rack – so our new travel plans would be unlikely to draw attention. The four of us had agreed not to meet up and travel together, but to leave home early and make our separate, less obvious journeys and then meet at the scooter rack. We even agreed to aim to get to school earlier than the start of the before-school activity club.

I was surprised to find my dad at the breakfast table when I came down. He was usually long gone by now, but today he was intently stirring his tea while my mum was at the stove doing the usual poached eggs. Neither of them commented on my early arrival, on the fact that I was dressed, or on the neatly packed school bag over my shoulder. I was either in big trouble about something or I'd interrupted a conversation they didn't want me to hear.

I thought it a good idea to change the subject and try to impress them before they got in first with whatever was on their minds. "We're doing this massive project at school. Just Arthur, Eric, Victor and me. About Earnest Shackleton, the polar explorer. He had a ship called the *Endurance* and Mr Hetherington says we can do displays and presentations and everything. It could turn out to be a model project."

"You're going to make a model?" said my dad without looking up from his tea.

"No – well we might – no, Mr Hetherington means that the project will probably be so good that other kids will model their work on ours, like, imitate what we've done. We'll be setting them an example!"

"That'll make a change,' said my mother without turning round.

"Anyway, I said I'd be early so that we could start on the research, so could I just have a piece of toast and some juice, please?"

"No! You'll have your poached egg."

"Dad! Tell her to let me go."

"Just you wait till you're older. Then you won't be talking about letting things go!" And he got up, with his tea, and went into the family room to watch breakfast television.

"You and your big mouth," said my mother as she placed the poached egg on toast in front of me and left to sit by my father in the living room.

What was that about? Sometimes parents talk in code. Their responses were a mystery, but at least they didn't mention Henley Phipps or anything to do with attempted murder – so I shovelled down the egg and toast and before they could accuse me of anything else, called a cheery goodbye and ran out to my waiting scooter.

What I usually like about the early morning on a school day is the way everyone seems to be going somewhere. It's purposeful. It feels organised. Everyone seems to know what they're doing. In the holidays and at weekends everyone seems a bit aimless, driving round in circles looking for a shop to go to and bumping into one another.

I scooted off down Pineapple Road towards the junction with Artichoke Avenue. A lot of the roads on our estate were named after fruit and vegetables for some reason: probably so that kids would be embarrassed having to say the name of their road out loud when the teacher was filling in the register at the beginning of the school year. Whatever, people called it the 'five-a-day' estate.

I felt – brillig – and was just wondering as I turned into Artichoke Avenue whether my mum and dad would let me change my first name to Ernest – or even Shackleton when I saw them! Kids. Hundreds of them – well, thirty at least – standing in clumps on either side of the road.

When they saw me, I heard various shouts of, "He's here! He's here! Henley, he's here!"

I couldn't turn back. I had to go for it.

Henley was nowhere in sight among the crowds of expectant kids so I just went. Head down, back bent, right foot pounding the ground and the scooter speeding and bumping off the pavement into the centre of the road. The kids were screaming for Henley now and I just caught a glimpse of his furious head above the crowd as I passed. He was roaring for them to get out of the way and pushing his way through. Cars were honking, drivers were swearing, kids were screaming and just as I cleared the last of the crowds, I turned and saw Henley grabbing somebody's scooter and making a wobbly attempt to give chase.

Cars had stopped in the road. Kids were running after Henley, not wanting to miss the final confrontation, and just as I was feeling that I was going to make it into the safety of school, my right shoe flew off and was left lying in the middle of the road as I careered on; it was as though I'd run out of petrol or my chain had come off and I was losing speed. Still free- wheeling down Artichoke Avenue, towards the point where it meets Russet Close,

How Many Times Do I Have to Tell You?

where out school is, I made one last supreme effort to hit the ground with my right shoeless foot.

At the third push - "Owwww!!" My sock was torn off by the rough tarmac and the shock to my uncovered foot caused me to jerk my steering to one side. The scooter stalled and spun, wheel over handle bars, catapulting me head first into the hedge and before I could open my eyes and properly work out whether or not I was fatally injured, something heavy crashed into my scooter and me.

Two scooters, intertwined. Mine and the one Henley had been riding. No sign of Henley.

Eric, Arthur and Victor were suddenly there pulling me out of the hedge.

"My shoe!" I groaned.

Arthur held my shoe in front of me, "Retrieved. And your sock," smiling so much that all you could see was mouth and teeth.

"Henley! Where is he?"

Eric, Arthur and Victor, turned the corners of their mouths down, made their eyes very big and just pointed over the hedge into the conservation area.

"Can you stand up?" said Victor. "You need to go to the medical room with your foot."

"Have I still got a foot?"

"Just about. Come on."

As we hobbled towards school – surrounded by jostling kids trying to see how injured I was – Victor said, "Henley found that pond in the conservation area, by the way. I think he's still in there now."

"Thinking about doing a science project on pond life," said Eric.

As we approached the school's main entrance, Mr Nixon came striding out followed by Mr Hetherington and Mrs Ditchfield.

"You three get into school." Eric, Arthur and Victor just stood there. "Now!" bellowed Mr Nixon, making Mrs Ditchfield jump. My three friends hurried away.

"Mr Hetherington, please take McConkey to the medical room."

I was trying to look seriously injured by this time: wobbling, grimacing, biting my lip to show how much pain I was in, making barely controlled groaning noises in my chest and rolling my eyes as though I was about to faint.

"Mrs Ditchfield, there seems to be a wet boy out there in the conservation area. Would you mind?" Mrs Ditchfield hurried away, importantly.

"I'll be all right, sir. I just need to put my sock and shoe on," I said stoically to Mr Hetherington. I was actually thinking I didn't want to go into the medical room in case they brought Henley Phipps there.

That would be a catastrophe!

So he sent me on to the classroom. On the way Jennifer Greenhouse appeared, carrying a register. "Did you hear about Henley in the pond? No reflection, nothing. Loads of kids saw it, I mean didn't see it, but loads of kids did. *Nothing* in the water! He's definitely a vampire. That's proof, that is!" She hurried away.

Ten minutes later I was recovering in the book corner of our classroom when Mr Nixon came in. "Good thinking, Mr Hetherington," he said loudly, so that all the class could hear. "Mr McConkey will be in isolation until I've had a chance to see his parents about his behaviour. It may interest you all to know that Henley Phipps has had to go home – and not just because of his wet clothes!"

Every single face in the class turned to look at me with such foreboding that even the prospect of a whole day in the book corner couldn't subdue the awful churning in my stomach.

****

12

How Many *More* Times Do I Have to Tell You?

"What does Mr Nixon want to see me and your dad about?"

"How should I know?"

"If you don't know, I don't know who does!"

"Well, I don't. You'll have to ask him. He should know."

"You're getting too cheeky, you are! Go to bed."

"It's only five o'clock!"

"You should have thought about that before."

"Before what?"

"Bed!"

"What about tea?"

"You'll get your tea when I say so. Now get!"

It was all so unjust! I get bullied repeatedly by Henley Phipps and end up being blamed. I know, there was the bow and arrow incident, but with everything else, I've been the put-upon one, the innocent victim. That safety razor business wasn't me. The scooter crash wasn't me. His wet clothes wasn't me – and what about my foot? I might have to go to hospital and end up with a limp forever; and what is even worse, my mum and dad will go on about it forever. Why do I always get blamed? Why does Henley always get away with everything? They might as well wrap him up in bubble-wrap for all the blame he ever gets. They don't even ask him questions. I bet my life is going to be ruined now. Mr Hetherington will go funny and won't let me do the Shackleton project, all my friends will be stopped from playing with me, Nixon will invent tortures for me for years and I might even get moved off the top table for literacy. Out of spite! I might as well just jump out of my bedroom window now and smash onto the hard paving stones below. Just to show them. Then they'd be sorry. People would put flowers by our gate with messages on them like, 'Why does no one ever listen?'

"Your tea's ready."

"I don't want any."

"It's pasta."

I went downstairs trying to look as hurt as possible.

The next day at school no sign again of Henley Phipps and I had to stay in isolation until my parents came for the meeting after school. At least I was allowed to read and to go on the computer and find stuff out about Shackleton, but I wasn't allowed to go out at play or talk to any of my friends. Trapped on this unforgiving ice-flow, I started to copy out Shackleton McConkey's diary:

This uninhabited island, with its harsh mountains looming through the swirling cloud and thick glaciers tumbling to the coast, would not be the final resting place for my men. I knew I had to rescue them…

Mrs. Ditchfield came in with my lunch at one o'clock and then, no one.

I reassured them that whilst there was breath in my body, I would not let them perish. Whilst I knew some of them were inwardly despairing, they listened attentively, with hope in their eyes, to my final plan.

Immediately I concluded the speech, my brave comrades cheered despite their failing strength and once more this galvanized me to action.

Tomorrow, I will begin my journey to rescue these loyal shipmates, who had put their faith in me. I am determined to not let them down!

And so the day passed.

At half past three, my mother came into school on her own. My dad hadn't made it back from the job he was on. She looked over-awed. Mr. Nixon sat her down in his office with me alongside her and him behind his desk.

"I'm sorry Mr. McConkey couldn't come. He's still somewhere on the motorway and work is – er – quite difficult at the moment."

"These things happen, Mrs. McConkey. These things happen. You're here anyway. I'm sorry to have to ask you in but we're all getting a bit worried about Jimmy."

I winced. I'm not Jimmy, *I'm Jim!* I bet Shackleton never got called, Ernie!

He went on to talk about me as though I wasn't there. How I'd tried to embarrass my teacher with a safety razor, how I'd denied everything despite the evidence, how I lived in a fantasy world, how I was obsessed with people's first names, how I was a ringleader drawing other boys into undesirable ways including reciting the Jabberwocky poem at every opportunity and bringing heavy goods vehicles into every conversation, how my work was suffering because of my challenging behaviour (he was making that up, my work was fine); how "we were hoping for all round SATs Level 6's but now...?"; how I was going out of my way to implicate a perfectly innocent and vulnerable older boy in my misdemeanors and how, to top it all, I had caused a major incident outside the school with scooters leading to damage of person and property.

What did he mean, 'vulnerable'? Henley Phipps?

Mr. Nixon took a moment to catch breath and wipe his handkerchief across his shiny head.

My mother looked at me. "Is this true?"

"Which part?"

"All of it!"

"No. Not all of it."

"Some of it's true then."

"Not really. It depends how you look at it. It's more complicated than that."

"I think I'll have to stop his computer games," said my mother, obviously casting about to find a response to this deluge of accusations.

"We find cutting down on sugar intake helps, fruit drinks, chocolate…" said Mr Nixon trying to sound like a doctor.

"Oh, definitely! No more Thursday chocolate for you, my lad!"

My dad brought me chocolate on a Thursday. His pay day.

"Who are these other boys you mentioned?"

"Well, you can rest assured that his group of close friends will be fine once James modifies his behaviour. The one I'm really worried about is Henley Phipps."

"Yes I know about Henley. I work at the optician's in Lime Avenue – so – I know…"

Mr Nixon looked relieved. "I'm glad, I'm glad. You'll know about Henley's…" he said tailing off. "James seems to have taken against him in a major way. To the point where it looks like a vendetta, which in the circumstances, confidential circumstances…suffice to say, he could do without scooters and being thrown into ponds just at the moment."

"You threw him into a pond?"

"No!"

"How could you throw him into a pond? I know his mother, Mr Nixon. She lives by the Lime Avenue shops where I work in the mornings. I talk to her sometimes. I think James and I ought to go round and have a word with her – and Henley."

"What?"

"You'll do as you're told. How many times have I told you about ponds?"

"What?"

All mum said on the way home was, "I could do without this!"

There was a grass verge just outside our house and sitting on it were Victor, Arthur and Eric.

"Are these the kids you're leading into bad ways?" my mother said as we drew closer. "It's no good you lot talking to this one. He's a marked man. A bad influence. You'd better get off home before your parents find out about him."

"He's been misjudged, Mrs McConkey," said Victor. "The fates have conspired against him."

"The what?"

"He's been very unlucky, that's all. Fate – you know?"

"I'll give him unlucky. It's very unlucky that he's going to bed without any tea. It's very unlucky that I've got to go and grovel to Mrs Phipps. It's very unlucky that his dad's going to find out what he's really like when he could really do without it!"

With that my mother swept on down our path.

"Mrs Phipps?" said Arthur. "Have you got to talk to her as well?"

"Victor, I'd like you to read this extract from Shackleton McConkey's diary, I said trying to hold myself together and handing him my notebook.

Puzzled, Victor read:

At 5pm a movement in the ship observed from camp lookout. The funnel collapsed & the stern after rearing high in the air disappeared below the ice - the last of the crushed hull of the Endurance. From the time the ice opened she sank in 10 minutes.

"She sank in ten minutes," I repeated, "and my brave comrades cheered me despite their failing strength and once more this galvanized me to action."

"Are *we* sunk?" said Arthur bottom lip beginning to quiver ever so slightly.

"It's going to be a long old journey back to civilization," said Victor.

****

13

Multiplex Showdown

The next day was Saturday. I was supposed to be going to the pictures in the afternoon with Victor, Eric and Arthur. Eric's mum was going to pick us all up at lunch time, drop us off while she went shopping and then collect us at the end.

No one came.

"I thought you were going to the pictures?" My mother.

"I'm meeting everybody there."

"Mind you do. I don't want you there on your own. You're in enough trouble as it is."

"Eric's mum will be there. She's taking us. She said to wait by where they sell the tickets."

Great mates! They might have to stick up for me and where are they? A chance to defend an innocent man and they're off. I'm like the lone sheriff standing up to the baddies and the whole town is hiding behind their curtains and keeping out of the way. The music is ominous again and the clock is ticking and I'm heading into town on the bus, alone, friendless – and just heartbreakingly brave.

The film had already started when I got there. No sign of anyone I knew and I had to find a seat in the dark. Up near the back. I could tell from the general noise that the whole place was full of kids – laughing too hard whenever something funny happened in the film and then going over the top whenever anything scary or exciting happened.

It was quite a good film and I was just forgetting that I was on my own and the sword of doom was hanging over me when I heard –

"GERBIL! I known you're in here. I'm coming to get you, Gerbil. You've really, really had it now, Gerbil."

Phipps!

A huge voice! It drowned the forced laughter and the whole audience was silenced. Not a sound, not a movement. The film carried on while everyone just froze.

Pause.

Then, down at the front, some kids jumped out of their seats, screaming – then the group next to them exploded out of their seats – and the next – and the next. He was *crawling along the floor grabbing legs – looking for ME!!*

He was working his way up, row by row. Surely he couldn't get to me. There were too many rows, too many seats, too many people. Kids just kept leaping out of their seats screaming – "Ow! Get off! Ahhhhh!" None of the grown-ups who ran the place was anywhere to be seen and the ones who were sitting there with their kids just seemed to ignore what was going on. He was getting closer and closer.

I tucked my legs up under me on the seat, hoping that when he got to me he'd think it was an empty seat – and then he was there at the end of my row and I could hear him.

"Gerbil – Gerbil …I know you're here – I'm coming for you – you cannot escape, Gerbil." And then he was there – on the floor – just to my right. A big red face (with some nasty scratches on it) peering out of the darkness, looking up at me like some troll from under a bridge.

"Heh, heh, heh – look who's here! I'm going to bite your head off, McConkey. Right through your neck with my great big shiny teeth!"

There was nowhere to go. He would grab my legs and pull me down into the darkness and … I squeezed away from him as far back into the seat as I could. His hand flapped over the edge of the seat trying to find a bit of me to take hold of – then his face – that terrible scarred, leering face – rearing up. I pulled back by leg – and – kicked. I didn't plan it. It was a reflex action. I kicked at him with all my might and my foot thumped into his face.

Oh no – what have I done? Again!! A pause and then –

An agonised splutter: "My teeth! You had my teeth out! My teeth! You've got my teeth!"

Two large hands took hold of Henley Phipps's collar from behind and yanked him backwards away from me towards the aisle – it was one of the attendants – holding on for grim life as Henley clutched his face and screamed, "My teeth! He's had my teeth!" And off into the distance. A plaintive, miserable cry echoing up the aisle, through the foyer and out into the street, –'My teeth – my teeeeeeth!".

Had I really kicked his front teeth out? I'm sure they were his grown-up teeth as well, not his baby teeth. They'd never grow again! Would he be back any minute with a policeman or worse than that, his mother?

I had to escape – melt into the surrounding streets incognito – invisible. Carefully, I unravelled my legs and placed them on the floor beneath the seat. *There was something stuck to the sole of my shoe! Something lumpy and wet and sticky!*

Henley Phipps's front teeth!

I knew what was going to happen. He'd be waiting for me out in the street. With a great big black hole where his front teeth should have been; there would be bright red, livid, scratches all down his face and his arms would be flailing about in agony as he tried in vain to make his mouth say how much he hated me and was going to get me. It was all over and I hadn't even had a chance to say goodbye to my mum and dad – and my friends – or even Mr Nixon.

The film ended. Everyone left and I sat there. Perhaps I could give him his teeth back and he could take them to the dentist and have them put back in? Then his mum might not notice. How could I walk out with somebody's dripping teeth stuck into the bottom of my foot? They weren't my teeth; how could I even touch them?

I had to face him.

Ray Speakman

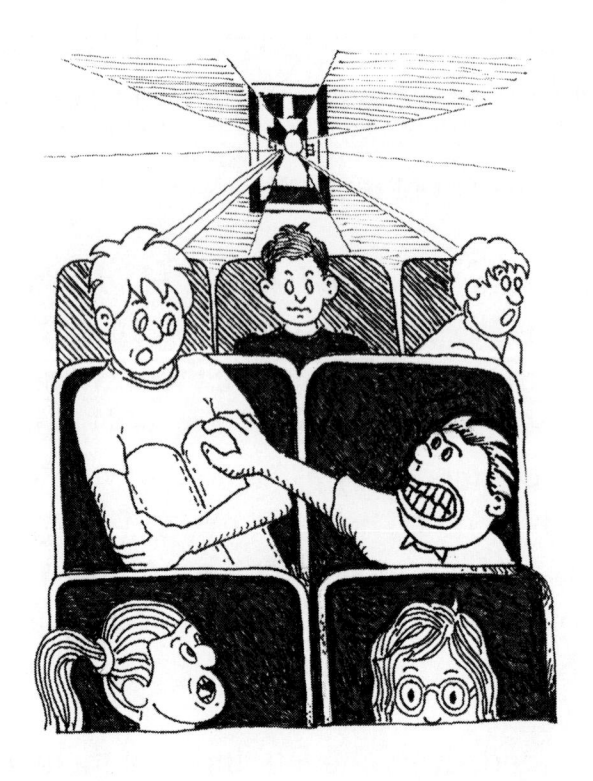

I had a plan – you never know, it might work.

So – carefully – very slowly I walked gingerly, just touching my heel to the floor outof the dark into shiny, bright, wet daylight. It was pouring down. And there, on the wet pavements - nobody. Just me, an empty cinema and the rain. And the teeth stuck into the sole of my shoe. Think – think – I can't walk through town like this. They might break – or I might lose them. I had a hanky. So – with one hand I leaned against the cinema doors and with the hanky – I reached down and took the teeth from my foot and into the hanky. They were stuck hard, but in the end, they let my foot go.

All the way home I held them in my hanky, my arm stretched out in front of me. Walking. On the bus. Into my house. Up to the bathroom. Sit on the toilet. Open the hanky. Eyes crunched up. Squeezing my nostrils shut. Not breathing. And they were there in my hanky, in my hand.

Plastic teeth! Plastic vampire teeth!

I put them down the toilet and flushed it. They wouldn't go down but just lay there under the water, leering up at me like a great big Henley Phipps grin! So I put my hand into the toilet bowl (gross! gross!), wrapped them in about twenty layers of toilet paper and pulled the plug again. Gone – but I knew I could never, ever, go to the toilet again without thinking that Henley Phipps's teeth might come popping up out of the water screaming – 'Oi, I want hold of you!' – just before sinking those horrible sharp fangs into my bum!

****

14

Hard Times

'Why aren't you out of bed?' My mother again – poised to rip the bedclothes off. "And what's happened to the brand new toilet roll I've just put in the bathroom?"

I pointed down my throat and mimed, "I can't talk".

I couldn't talk mainly because I couldn't begin to explain what had been going on with Henley Phipps and his teeth – especially if they suddenly popped up again in the toilet bowl. I came up with an illness which would:

1. Let me stay in bed for as many days as possible.

2. Make it so I wouldn't have to answer too many questions.

I thought of going into a coma – but didn't think I could keep it up. So it had to be tonsillitis which I was prone to, as my mother would say.

'What? What are you saying? Light what? You don't need the light on. It's morning.'

I croaked, "Tonsillitis. In my tonsils."

"Not again!" She felt my forehead and agreed. I *was* ill. Was I? This was slightly worrying but - I would have to stay in bed, eat sloppy food such as ice cream and custard, (I could do that) and read (I could do that too). You don't need your voice to read and reading is a well-known cure for tonsillitis and the fear of Henley Phipps.

He would be prowling the streets looking for me. I bet he didn't even have to say he wanted hold of me because everybody would know by now. They would scuttle into their houses and lock their doors. The streets would be empty except for a cold wind and the occasional plastic bag doing erratic somersaults along the pavement. I lay in bed imagining him, when it went dark, standing under the lamppost just by my house – waiting, hood up, hands in pockets, his shadow enlarged by the angle of the light from the lamppost so it stretched out down the whole length of the street. Looming. Threatening. Like one of those posters for a really scary film that you see on the side of a bus with the words, 'Terrifying!' and 'Chilling' jumping out at you as the bus groans its way down the street.

"We need to talk to you." It was my mum and my dad coming into the bedroom.

"Why?" I sat up, went red and this thumping noise started in my head – I think it was all the excuses I could think of rushing into my brain ready to be used to explain whatever it was they were going to accuse me of. Whatever Henley Phipps's mother or Mr Nixon had told them on the phone, perhaps, but I hadn't heard the phone! Eric's mum confessing that she hadn't taken me to the pictures so I must have gone without a grown-up. The teeth in the toilet! Oh no, not the teeth in the toilet! Or had they found the bow and oil-stained arrow?

"Why?" I said a second time remembering to croak this time and wince at the pain of having to say something.

My mum and dad sat either side of me on the bed and talked. *It wasn't about me*! It was always about me. How could it not be about me? It was about them. My dad had packed in his job. He couldn't do it anymore he said, the long hours, the driving, and the uncertainty, the nightmares, the broken sleep – it was all making him ill and the doctor had said, more than once, that he ought to think about doing something else. So he had let the job go.

"I'm really sorry, Jim."

I was taken aback. He was saying sorry to me!

"I'm thinking of seeing about going back to painting and decorating. You know, I served my time at it as an apprentice."

He *had* told me this - quite a few times. "I know," I said.

My mother was practical about it. "We're going to have to go careful. I know money's short as it is, and I never have a penny after a Tuesday, but from now on it's going to be really short. We're going to have to cut back."

"I'll give up going to the pictures!" I said enthusiastically – forgetting to croak.

"Good lad," said my dad, "and your mum is going try for a little job up at the school – in the kitchens. She'll be able to keep an eye on you – if she gets it. If she takes it, I mean."

They smiled.

"It would fit in with the job at the optician's. I'd do early morning at the school. Apparently the school only wants someone to help with the preparation – I wouldn't be serving and showing you up. That means I could leave when your dinner time starts and be at the optician's in plenty of time. I was getting bored with the mornings at home anyway. Mind, you'll have to pull your weight as well, in the house, if I'm going to be out more. Help me with the jobs in the house and the shopping."

"Course I will."

"Good lad." My dad nodded and rose to leave.

"Oh yes – I meant to tell you," said my mother. "I saw Mrs Phipps coming out of the optician's this morning. They were keeping it quiet, but now she thinks people should know. Henley had an eye test with us a few weeks ago and he's been referred to the hospital. They're going to keep him in for tests. I said I'd tell you. I said I was sure you'd want to lend him one of your computer games or some books to take with him. I'll tell you two something - if you think we've got worries, think again!"

As they left, my dad turned and said, "That tonsillitis seems a lot better now. Why don't you get dressed and come down for your dinner – and - thanks."

"What for?"

"Not minding about me and the job. I'll find something. We won't be needing the Food Bank – for a bit, anyway!"

Henley Phipps in hospital for tests? What, vampire tests? Injuries sustained from falling off his bike or being submerged in a manky-school-pond tests? Perhaps he has water borne infections? Or mouth damage. Perhaps the doctor would hold up his x rays and say, "This shows major damage, caused, according to DNA residue, by someone called McConkey. Call the police, nurse."

My head thumped and buzzed as though a car alarm had gone off somewhere deep in my brain. Lend him one of my computer games? My mother going for a job up at the school! After the interview for the job, Mr Nixon would probably put his hand on her shoulder and say, "I'm really sorry, Mrs McConkey, but what with James and his recent behaviour – and with Henley Phipps touch and go in the hospital - I'm sure you'll understand …"

Just as the car alarm in my head reached maximum volume, my dad shouted, "Who's put something down this toilet? It's all blocked."

****

15

Victor

The only way I could make my head go quiet was to do jobs about the house. I'd offered to do some of my mum's knitting for her. She taught me how ages ago but had to stop when my dad started calling me Mary – as he always did when I knitted, or sewed or cooked. So I cleaned some windows instead, but wasn't allowed to stand on a chair or use the step ladders, which left the job half done, so went out and mowed the back lawn with this pathetic little electric lawn mower we had. It buzzed like my brain, making me wish that I could put all my worries on the compost with the grass cuttings.

Just as I was about to start on the edges of the grass with the big clippers, my dad leaned out of the kitchen window and shouted; "There's a girl here for you. A girl! She's got fantastically huge eyes!" he hissed. "Why don't you ask her to come in? You could show her how to knit – or – you could just hold hands and drown in her eyes…" and he started singing, 'Love is in the air' until I heard my mother tell him to shut up.

I said nothing. It wasn't worth it. I knew he would just escalate it if I tried to respond.

It was Victor. I closed the front door on the latch and we went and sat on our front wall. Pineapple Avenue was deserted.

Victor broke the silence. "Have you heard about Henley Phipps?"

"What's up with him?"

"Tests."

"Is it like an infection - or an injury – or what?"

"I don't know. I think they know at school but they're not saying." Pause. "Look, Jim, you've got to get this into perspective. It's almost certainly not because of the bow and arrow, or the scooter race, or the pond…"

"Or the vampire teeth!"

"The what?" I told her about the teeth. I didn't even ask her where they all were on that day, why they'd abandoned me. Things were complicated enough as it was.

"Aren't you going to ask why we didn't turn up at the multiplex?

Eric's mum's car had been hit by a lorry at a roundabout. It was too high and too long so it couldn't get round properly and crashed through the front of her car, where she was waiting to let it pass. The bonnet was all caved-in but they were all right – Eric and his mum, Arthur and Victor - except they had to wait for hours for a tow-truck. Eric would no doubt be re-enacting the incident for ever, going on and on about turning circles, heaving round the huge steering wheel, throwing his tangled red hair from side to side and screaming for everyone to brace themselves. They must have been a bit shaken though – the noise apart from anything else – and I hadn't even asked after them or tried to find out why they hadn't turned up.

As always, I'd assumed it was all about me, about me being let down, about me being left to face Henley Phipps alone, about the nightmare I was in, never thinking that other people have their own nightmares too.

"Soz, I didn't think to ask why you weren't at the cinema," I said, too uncomfortable to say the word 'sorry' properly.

"We think that Henley has something wrong with him that's nothing to do with what's been happening. We just haven't noticed. Maybe this is a chance for us to sort things out. Go and see him before he goes into hospital."

I didn't know what to say.

"You can't let things go on like this. Someone's got to make the first move, and I can't see it being him. I've heard that he goes into hospital on Friday. You collect your mum's food order from the shop on Thursday night, don't you, so why don't I meet you there, give you a hand and then we can call in to Henley's house on the way home? We could take him something, couldn't we? It would be like peace talks, wouldn't it? We could be diplomats!"

Pause. Her huge out-of- proportion eyes waiting for my answer.

"Has your tonsillitis come back, Jim? Shall I ask your mum for a drink of water?"

****

16

Mission disaster

I didn't have time to dwell on Thursday's diplomatic initiative with Henley. The week just piled up with things happening. My num got the job in the school kitchens; my dad started decorating the stairs and landing in order to practice his new career (when it happened); and the Shackleton project was going brilliantly. We were writing pretend postcards, letters and diary entries from the crew describing what we were doing while the *Endurance* was trapped in the ice; the best one was from me pretending to be Frank Hurley rescuing essential equipment from the waterlogged ship.

Arthur claimed that he had read somewhere on a website that Shackleton had found a frozen Jabberwocky in the ice and the only way we could get him to shut up about it was to ask Mr Hetherington if Arthur, Eric, Victor and I could do a reading of the Jabberwocky poem in assembly – as long as Arthur promised to move on afterwards from Lewis Carroll to Ernest Shackleton.

"Great idea, lads! What did you say you wanted to do?" Mr Hetherington very often got his sentences the wrong way round – even when he was clean shaven, which he was this week. He said he'd have to ask the Headteacher and Mr Nixon if it was okay, but he thought it would be okay and could we have it ready for Thursday – when it was Mr Hetherington's turn to do the afternoon assembly.

Then Eric discovered that they *did* have lorries at the time Shackleton went to Antarctica because it was 1915 when the First World War was on and they definitely had lorries in the First World War. Victor argued that there was no room on the *Endurance* for lorries, only sledges and dogs, there were no roads in Antarctica and anyway the ship was stuck in the ice and ended up sinking – so…

"Okay," said Eric, "No lorries."

Given that we stayed in at play and lunch, we had plenty of time to run through our reading of the Jabberwocky poem. What we decided was that Victor, Eric and I would read the actual poem and Arthur would translate the various unusual words for everyone. So, for instance, when we said 'slithy' he would explain that this word was made by combining 'slimy' and 'lithe', and that 'mimsy' was a combination of 'miserable' and 'flimsy'. Then we could encourage the children to make up their own words for things in the same way. For example the word 'scrage' which you might use to describe an injury to your skin would be a joining together of 'scratch' and 'rage' (to describe the raging pain you were in). I think we were all picturing at this moment.

"Isn't that an actual word?" said Eric.

"It is now," laughed Arthur.

So when Thursday afternoon came, it all went off quite well. A lot of kids laughed (as opposed to thinking we were mad) and even Mr Nixon laughed a bit, if you could call it a laugh: more like a *small* dog bark – as opposed to the *big* dog bark he does when you're in trouble.

Henley had not been in school all week, but then he suddenly appeared with his mother and they stood at the back of Thursday's afternoon assembly. At the end, Mr Hetherington drew everyone's attention to them standing there and everyone's head swivelled.

"It's very nice to welcome Mrs Phipps and Henley to the assembly today. Henley's off to hospital tomorrow, so I'm sure you'll all want to say, 'All the best, Henley'."

A slight pause, lots of encouraging nods from Mr Hetherington and then everyone said in that very slow way children have when they all speak at the same time: "Allll the besssst, Henleeeey."

Henley grinned and pointed at everyone and Mrs Phipps mouthed, "Thank you".

Shortly before tea time Victor and I loaded up my mum's food order at the Lime Avenue shops. I had a sort of trolley or truck that I'd made from some old push chair wheels and bits of wood. My dad had showed me how, said his granddad had showed him. It was ideal for the job. My mother used to write her order down in a little note book and leave it at the general shop and the man there would put it in cardboard boxes to be collected. My mum or dad usually picked it up depending on who had the car, but in these hard times at home (my dad was selling the car and it was already out in front of our house with a price, or nearest offer, stuck to the inside of the windscreen), I'd been given the job of collecting the weekly order for the foreseeable future.

Henley lived in the second of the two houses after the shops. They had very high privet hedges in front of them and a gate in the middle. Victor and I hadn't even planned what we were going to say, but it was understood that we would go and knock on Henley's door – and then just make it up as we went along.

We arrived at the front gate. I put my hand out to open it and it was wrenched out my hand from the inside. Henley! Fists clenched, head down, tongue between his teeth.

Victor shouted, "You can't fight, Henley! You're ill!"

"I'm not ill! Anyway, I'm not going to fight. I'm just going to…." He was obviously trying to think what he was going to do. "Is this your mother's stuff, Victoria?" he leered, kicking the trolley.

"Her name's Victor," I said trying not to look scared. "And anyway it's *my* mother's, not Victor's!"

"Good. Oh very, very good! Little Jimmy's doing his mummy's shopping! Let's just see if he's remembered everything."

With that he thrust his hand into the first of the boxes and pulled out a bag of sugar, said what it was and then punched it so that the bag burst. Then he took out a bottle of pop, shook it hard and then released the top so that it squirted high into the air. Then eggs, then bacon wrapped in paper, apples, frozen peas, biscuits, bread and potatoes all ripped from their packaging and scattered out into the road. More, and more and more. Cars honked as stuff rolled under their wheels and Victor and I simply shrank away trying not to be hit by flying food.

Then it was over. Henley, bent forward, right hand on his right knee, pointed at us, paused to gather some breath and said, "Shopping all done! Good work, team. Just think yourself lucky that I didn't fire arrows into it, or throw it into a pond, or kick it in the face...."

At that moment Mrs Phipps, brought out by the noise of car horns, appeared at the gate. She was horrified by what she found. "Who did this?" she said, looking along Lime Avenue as if expecting to see someone running away.

"I tried to stop them, mum: Jimmy and Victoria. They just went berserk – busting open packets, throwing stuff into the road and laughing like mad things. I couldn't believe it! It's really upset me, Mum - all that good food everywhere."

"Jimmy, what were you doing?"

All I could think to say was, "We just came round to see Henley. I brought some computer games and books for him to take to the hospital with him."

It was as though this was a play and everyone had forgotten their lines.

****

17

What did I tell you?

We salvaged what we could from the scattered shopping, mainly the things in tins. Everything else was ruined. Henley disappeared into his house followed by his mother, but then she emerged a few moments later with a broom and a bin bag and as she began clearing up said, "It's the hospital. On his mind, you know. Mind you, he seems more worried about the chipped tooth!"

Victor and I looked at each other. What chipped tooth?

We said nothing as we pulled the much depleted cargo of cardboard boxes back towards home. My mother opened the back door before I could get to it. Mrs Phipps must have been on the phone.

She just looked at the shopping, at Victor and then at me – and cried. She tried to stop herself, but then she just cried! She tried to set her face firm, but great big tears rolled everywhere.

"We haven't even got through the weekend, yet! Never mind next week", she said by way of explanation.

I pushed past her and up to my room shouting, "Nobody ever listens! What did I tell you? What did I tell you?"

"Come in, Victoria. You'd better tell me what's been going on."

****

18

It was the computer games.

"Your tea's ready."

I didn't want any tea, even if it was pasta. I didn't want any food ever again, especially as it was still only Thursday and we hadn't even got through the weekend. I bet my dad was off now seeing if he could get social services to give him a Food Bank voucher and it was my entire fault.

My mother didn't even come up to try and persuade me to come down. She just left me there. I couldn't read, I couldn't write, I couldn't draw. All I could think was, Shackleton survived hunger and cold for 635 days; he sailed 800 miles in a lifeboat and he brought all of his 28 men through their terrible ordeal alive. I wouldn't even last until Monday! I would probably never see my friends again. I would probably be found dead in my bedroom, starved and forgotten. Three days to Monday's school dinner! Eternity! I'll never make it.

The next thing I knew was that I'd fallen asleep and it was dark outside. Fading away already, too weak to resist sleep.

At the sound of voices from somewhere outside in the road, I managed to rouse myself enough to peak over my window sill and towards our front gate. There was a crowd there: Mrs Phipps, Victor, Eric, Arthur and all their parents with my mum and dad. They were talking and shaking hands and then, all except my parents, headed off up the road and into the night.

What had I done now? Had they found out something else? The chipped tooth, for instance. Henley was sick, obviously, dying possibly – no he couldn't be - and they'd found out that I'd made things worse by chipping his tooth in the pictures. I knew what would happen, my mother wouldn't even go, "How many times do I have to tell you?" She would go, "This time you've gone too far. That poor lad. I'm having you taken into care! See if Dr Barnardo can do anything with you!"

"Jim! Come down here." Pause, perhaps I could convince them I was asleep. "I know you're not asleep, I saw you at your bedroom window."

I swore.

"And there's no need to swear! Get down here."

I went down into the kitchen, scrunching my eyes against the light. The kitchen table was heaped high with groceries: eggs, vegetables, sugar, biscuits, bacon, meat, milk, pop, everything I'd lost and more.

"How did you do that?"

"I didn't. It was Victor. She went round and told your friends and they told their parents and they all went round to Mrs Phipps and they all went to the shops and then they all came here. But really it was you – taking those books round and the computer game."

"Mind you I thought giving him a game called *The Truth about Bats* was a bit risky after what I've heard you say about Henley being a vampire," said my dad.

"You've been unmasked, Jimmy."

"Jim!"

"Sit down. Jim. I need to tell you about Henley. His mother brought him to the optician's about a month ago. He'd been having blurred vision. The optician referred him to the hospital and now they're having him in the do some blood tests and scans. They think he's got a small blood clot just near his eye, which is pressing on his optic nerve and causing the blurred vision. If it goes into his brain it could be very serious. So they're going to do the tests and then, if they're right, try to treat it with medicine – and if that doesn't work, with an operation."

"It's serious then?"

"It could be."

"Oh. Do they know at school?"

"The school have been great all along, especially Mr Nixon, keeping an eye on him and that. And what you did with the books and the computer games has really impressed everybody. Your friend Victoria made sure we all knew what has been happening with you and Henley and how you did what you did despite what you must have felt about him. That's why they've given us all this food."

"The computer game was your idea, though."

"Only because I knew what Henley and his family were going through! You took it round to his house. You didn't know what was going on with Henley and his family yet you were still so - kind!"

"Yeah – well….You're not crying again are you? Don't cry, Mum. How many times do I have to tell you!"

****

19

A letter from Henley[3]

The Children's Hospital
Ward 20B

Dear Jim,

My Mum says I have got to write to you to say thank you for the computer games and the books. So thank you. The computer game is great but the books are not. I do not like reading. You should have known that. She said I had to tell you what was happening to me in hospital, so:

1. I have had a scan and some x-rays.

2. The scan was in this noisy tunnel which I thought was cool.

3. I think there are vampires here because they keep taking my blood away in tubes.

---

[3] This letter has been corrected for ease of reading. Henley's original is embarrassingly inaccurate and messy and I did not want you to think that Henley's mistakes were my (Jim's) mistakes. I hope that is clear.

4. They are going to do an operation because it is quicker and nicer than medicine. So they say. I think they have to peel part of my face off to get at the blood clot – which will leave a massive scar down behind my ear. Which will be COOL.

5. Then I'll be better but I didn't think I was sick before actually– except for the blurry eyes and a headache sometimes.

I think that when I come home you will have to let me join the lost names club because if you don't I will tell Nixon that you broke my tooth and then you will really be for it because I know for a fact that he bites kids and has some dead ones in his stockroom. But don't worry I will help you to get Eric to have a haircut and I will made Arthur stop saying mad words and I will tell Victoria that she's got to be a girl and not pretend any more.

And I will be the best friend you ever had.

Yours sincerely,
Henley

PS My mum has just gone and left me to lick the envelope. So I also want to say – just you wait, McConkey.

END

Thanks

Huge thanks go to: my wife, Chris, for her encouragement and impeccable proof-reading; Tony Turner, the actor who made such an impact with a first reading to children; Rachel and Stephen for laughing and being gripped; the teachers and children at Lightwoods School, Sandwell, UK and to Roy Mitchell, the television writer, for his suggestions and enthusiasm.